MY PICTURE DICTIONARY

Compiled by
Ellen Rudin and Marilyn Salomon

Pictures by
Elizabeth B. Rodger

A Golden Book • New York
Western Publishing Company, Inc.
Racine, Wisconsin 53404

Using Words

Human language is mostly words. People use words to speak to each other. They use words to write to each other. They use words to make signs for anyone to read. Of course it is possible sometimes for people to communicate without words. But using words makes communication easy and clear.

A dictionary is a special kind of book about words. It is called a reference book because it helps you look up words and find out what they mean. It gives the right way to spell words.

The words in this dictionary are arranged in alphabetical order so you can find them easily. Each word has a sentence that shows a way to use the word. Each word also has a picture that helps to explain it. You can look up a word you want to know. Or you can read the whole book and look at all the words and pictures.

There are many kinds of dictionaries. A person can have more than one kind. After you become older and need to know more about the uses of words, you may also own dictionaries that are longer and harder than this one.

acorn Patty found an **acorn** under the oak tree.

airplane The jet **airplane** flies above the clouds.

album Anita is looking at a photo **album** with her grandfather.

allowance Chris gets an **allowance** every week.

alphabet The **alphabet** begins with A and ends with Z.

apartment Tom can see the street from his **apartment**.

ankle Sally is sitting with one **ankle** crossed over the other.

apology An **apology** means showing that you are sorry.

ant A small **ant** can carry a big crumb.

aquarium Ralph feeds
the fish in his **aquarium**.

astronaut An **astronaut** wears
a space suit in space.

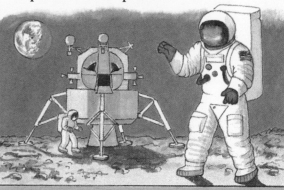

armchair Billy fell asleep
in the
armchair.

athlete An **athlete** needs
to be strong.

artist The **artist** is painting
Diane's portrait.

awning Joyce keeps cool
under the **awning**.

Bb

baby Everybody was a **baby** once.

backyard Tomatoes are growing in the **backyard**.

bakery Nancy's birthday cake came from a **bakery**.

banana Louis likes sliced **banana** on his cereal.

barn Cows live in a **barn**.

basket Red Riding Hood carried a **basket** of goodies to grandmother.

beak Every bird has a **beak**.

bench There is no room on the **bench** for Eric.

bicycle Mary rides her **bicycle** to school.

blanket George uses an extra **blanket** when it is cold.

bracelet An identification **bracelet** has a person's name on it.

breakfast We eat **breakfast** in the morning.

brick Every **brick** in the brick wall is red.

bridge There is a **bridge** over the river.

buckle The watch strap fastens with a **buckle**.

bully No one wants to be friends with a **bully**.

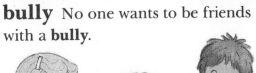

cafeteria There are long tables in the **cafeteria**.

cage The canary is flying back to its **cage**.

cake Janet is eating the first piece of the **cake**.

camera Greg uses his **camera** to take a picture.

campfire The campers sing songs around the **campfire**.

car The **car** needs gas.

carousel The **carousel** goes around and around to music.

chest The doctor is examining Donald's **chest**.

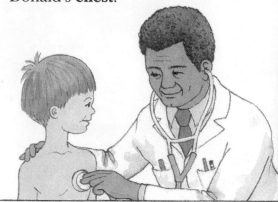

chicken A chicken lays eggs.

circus There are acrobats in the **circus**.

clock What time does the **clock** say?

chimney Smoke is coming out of the **chimney**.

cloud A **cloud** covered the sun.

coin Gina puts one **coin** in her bank every night.

comb Barbara's **comb** has big teeth and little teeth.

confetti Everyone threw **confetti** at the bride and groom.

copycat A **copycat** does what others do.

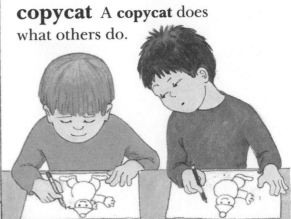

corner The traffic light is at the **corner**.

costume Tad has a frog **costume** for the play.

cow Milk comes from a **cow**.

cupboard Chris is putting the dishes in the **cupboard**.

cowlick The barber is trimming Sam's **cowlick**.

curb This **curb** has a step and a ramp.

crying Crying sometimes helps you feel better.

curly Lucy has naturally **curly** hair.

Dd

dance Dennis did a tap **dance** in assembly.

dandelion You can wish on a **dandelion**.

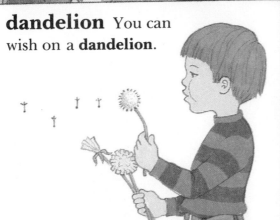

danger A **danger** sign means watch out.

dentist Patty goes to the **dentist** for checkups.

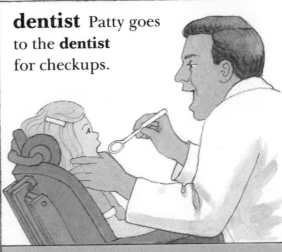

design The wallpaper has a **design** of boats.

dictionary
Sandy looks up hard words in the **dictionary**.

dimple Cary has a **dimple** in his chin.

dirt Skipper likes to play in the **dirt**.

dive Eric knows how to **dive**.

donut Anita went to the **donut** store.

dozen She bought a **dozen** donuts.

COUNTRY DONUTS

drawer One **drawer** is open.

drumstick Tim hits the drum with a **drumstick**.

duck A **duck** has webbed feet.

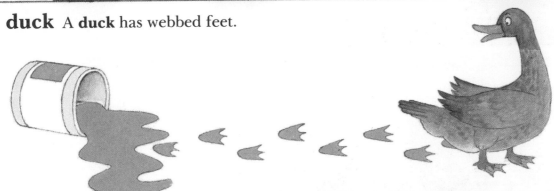

dump truck The **dump truck** is dumping sand.

Ee

ear Kevin holds the telephone receiver next to his **ear**.

earmuffs **Earmuffs** keep your ears warm.

earth Earthworms live in the **earth**.

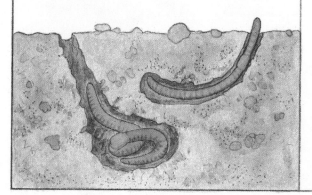

eat Joyce likes to **eat** peanut-butter sandwiches.

egg An **egg** has a thin shell.

elbow Your arm bends at the **elbow**.

elevator The **elevator** is full.

escalator Hold on to the rail of the **escalator**.

envelope Robert licks the **envelope** to seal it shut.

exercise Louis lifts weights for **exercise**.

erase It is Sally's turn to **erase** the board.

eyeglasses Everyone in Sharon's family wears **eyeglasses** except Skipper.

F f

face Susan has freckles on her **face**.

faucet Turn off the **faucet**.

fall Leaves **fall** in the Fall.

fence The cat went through a hole in the **fence**.

family There is a new person in George's **family**.

ferry A **ferry** takes people to the Statue of Liberty.

flag There is a **flag** on the ferry.

flashlight Mary is using a **flashlight**.

fog It is hard to see in the **fog**.

fox The **fox** lives in the forest.

frankfurter Some other names for **frankfurter** are hot dog, wiener, and weenie.

friend Mark is Judy's good **friend**.

frog A **frog** can jump very far.

furniture The movers are carrying **furniture**.

furry Rabbits and kittens are **furry** animals.

Gg

garage One car is in the **garage**.

garden Janet grows daffodils in her **garden**.

glass Daddy pours milk into a tall **glass**.

globe Eric is looking for Africa on the **globe**.

gloves Colleen has red woolen **gloves**.

glue Glue is messy.

goggles The worker is wearing **goggles** over his eyes.

group A **group** of campers are waiting for the bus.

grownup The chair holds one **grownup** or two children.

grapes Bunches of **grapes** are in the fruit bowl.

grasshopper A **grasshopper** landed on the picnic blanket.

guard This **guard** is at Buckingham Palace.

Hh

haircut Tad needs a **haircut**.

hamburger A **hamburger** with cheese on it is called a cheeseburger.

hand Barbara has five fingers on each **hand**.

handle You hold or carry something by the **handle**.

haystack A **haystack** is a stack of hay.

heart Tim can feel his own **heart** beating.

helmet It's a lucky thing that Patty wore a **helmet**.

helper Rover is a good **helper**.

hoe The gardener breaks up the soil with a **hoe**.

holiday What **holiday** was started by the Pilgrims and the Indians?

home Skipper's **home** is in the backyard.

hook The jacket is hanging on a **hook**.

hose The fire fighters are carrying a big **hose**.

hug Lucy gives her baby sister a **hug**.

hurt Donald **hurt** his arm.

hungry The puppies are **hungry** for their supper.

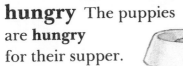

I i

iceberg The ship is sailing past an **iceberg**.

ice cream The **ice cream** is dripping down the cone.

idea A hike was a bad **idea**.

ice skates Gina is lacing her **ice skates**.

immediately Marilyn opened her present **immediately**.

individual Ten **individual** colors of paint are in the paintbox.

invention Television is one kind of **invention**.

initials The **initials** for United States of America are U.S.A.

iron A hot **iron** smoothes wrinkles out of clothes.

inside The cupcake has a cream filling **inside**.

island The house on the **island** is white.

J j

jacket Patty's **jacket** has deep pockets.

jack-o'-lantern A pumpkin can be made into a **jack-o'-lantern**.

jar Ralph needs help to open the **jar** of nuts.

jealous Bruce is **jealous**.

jeans Donna's **jeans** shrank.

joke Everyone laughed at the **joke**.

juggle The clown knows how to **juggle**.

juice Mommy is squeezing oranges to make orange **juice**.

jungle Many different animals live in the **jungle**.

junk Kevin keeps a lot of **junk** under his bed.

Kk

keep Sally has a new book to **keep**.

kangaroo Mama **kangaroo** carries her baby in her pouch.

ketchup Ketchup is good on French fries.

kayak A **kayak** is a little boat for one person.

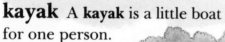

kettle The **kettle** whistles when the water boils.

key Chris wears his house **key** around his neck.

kitchen The **kitchen** is a place to cook food.

King Kong The star of the movie is **King Kong**.

kite A **kite** flies best on a windy day.

knapsack Joan's **knapsack** is slipping down.

kneel Sandy had to **kneel** to look under the chair.

knees Billy's shorts come to his **knees**.

knife A butter **knife** is not sharp.

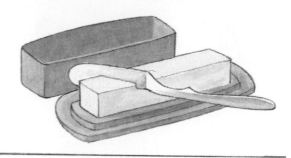

knot Tom tied his shoelaces in a tight **knot**.

knuckles Your fingers bend at the **knuckles**.

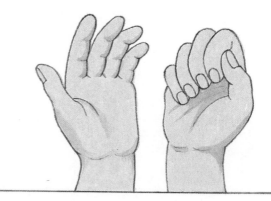

Ll

ladder Diane climbed the **ladder** to the top bunk.

leader The **leader** goes first.

lamp The **lamp** is shining.

laundry Greg took clean socks from the basket of dry **laundry**.

leash Rover wears a **leash** outdoors.

letter Is there a **letter** for me?

lifeguard A **lifeguard** must watch all the time.

library card A **library card** lets you take out books.

lick Kitty likes to **lick** her paw.

lighthouse The light from a **lighthouse** guides ships.

litter Who left all this **litter**?

loaf Karen is slicing a **loaf** of bread.

locker Henry keeps his sneakers in his **locker**.

lizard A **lizard** has a long tail.

lunchbox Joyce has a **lunchbox** with a Thermos.

Mm

machine Nancy won a prize from the gum **machine**.

magician A **magician** does tricks.

magnet Things made of metal stick to a **magnet**.

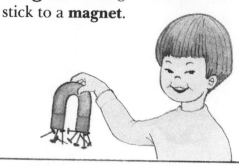

mailbox Sam's little brother can't reach the **mailbox**.

map The **map** shows where the treasure is buried.

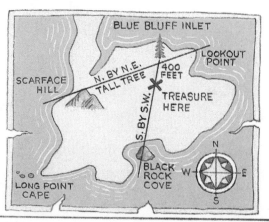

market Robert is buying
two lamb chops in the **market**.

mattress Jane thinks
her new **mattress**
is too hard.

medicine Sharon takes
her **medicine**
to get better.

mean Louis won't share his candy.
He's **mean**.

melt The butter is starting to **melt**.

middle-size Mother Bear is **middle-size**.

mosquito bite A **mosquito bite** itches.

mirror Kate sees all of herself in a three-way **mirror**.

moving van A **moving van** is in front of Martha's house.

mop Jerry used a **mop** to clean up the spilled milk.

music Donald and Donna play **music** on their recorders.

Nn

nap Mary's baby brother still takes a **nap**.

napkin Tad folded each birthday **napkin** like a little hat.

neat Pam is messy and Larry is **neat**.

needle A **needle** is used for sewing.

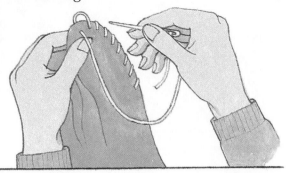

neighbor Our **neighbor** has a big dog.

nest There are three small birds in the **nest**.

never Gary **never** goes anywhere without his fuzzy blanket.

newspaper Billy is delivering a **newspaper**.

nickname Elizabeth's **nickname** is Betsy.

night light The **night light** stays on all night long.

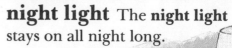

notebook Barbara has a looseleaf **notebook** for school.

oars Ken and Joyce row the boat with **oars**.

off The lights are **off**.

on A light is **on**. Can you see Mark in the window?

orchard Juicy red apples grow in the **orchard**.

ornament The star is Susan's favorite Christmas **ornament**.

overalls Scott has new striped **overalls** with a hammer loop.

outdoors Rain makes it wet **outdoors**.

overnight The snow fell **overnight**.

oven Pizza bakes in the **oven**.

owl An **owl** flies in the dark.

P p

package Frank bought a little **package** of cookies.

page Chapter Two starts on **page** 17.

pajamas Carla is wearing shortie **pajamas**.

parade Bruce saw the Thanksgiving Day **parade** in person.

parent A **parent** is a mother or a father.

partner Greg is Lucy's dancing **partner**.

patch Daddy's sweater has a **patch** on each elbow.

pebble A **pebble** is a tiny stone.

path Kevin shoveled a **path** through the snow.

pedal On a hill you have to **pedal** harder.

peek Hide your eyes and don't **peek**!

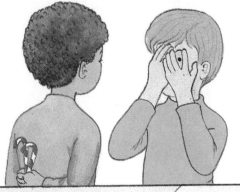

pitcher Gina fills the **pitcher** with water.

plant Gina pours the water on the **plant**.

play The children are putting on a **play**.

pocket Jane's skirt has a **pocket** in front.

police officer
One **police officer** is wearing sunglasses.

pond
How many ducks are in the **pond**?

porch
Henry's bicycle is on the **porch**.

postcard
Phillip wrote a **postcard** every day from camp.

Dear Mom and
      Dad
Went on a hike this
morning. Went
swimming later.
I can dive now.
I have a new friend.
His name is Tom.
We have fun.
   Love Phillip

POST CARD

Mr. and Mrs.
            Clarke
Old Mill Road
Greenville,
   Ohio

president Brenda was elected class **president**.

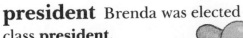

puppy Judy is choosing a **puppy**.

pretend The girls like to **pretend** they are astronauts.

purse A **purse** holds money.

price What is the **price** of one pretzel?

PRETZELS 2 FOR $1.00

puzzle Robert can't find an important piece of the **puzzle**.

Q q

question Anita has a **question**.

quiet The class is **quiet** so they can hear Anita's question.

quarrel Roy and Eric are having a **quarrel** about who won the race.

quilt It is cozy under the **quilt**.

quarter The candy machine takes a **quarter**.

quintuplets Emilie, Annette, Yvonne, Cecile, and Marie were famous **quintuplets**.

Rr

rabbit The **rabbit** hopped away.

racquet Diane swung the **racquet** and missed.

rainbow A **rainbow** came out after the sun-shower.

raisin A **raisin** is a dried grape.

rake Steven helps Mommy **rake** the leaves.

ranger The forest **ranger** watches for fires.

record Patty likes to hear the same **record** again and again.

rind Watermelon has a thick **rind**.

refrigerator Bruce ate all the leftovers in the **refrigerator**.

ring Janet is wearing a **ring** with her birthstone.

road sign Grace can read every **road sign**.

robot George wishes he had a **robot** to help him.

roller skates Beth speeds along on her **roller skates**.

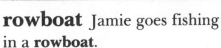

rocking chair Kitty loves the **rocking chair**.

rowboat Jamie goes fishing in a **rowboat**.

Ss

saddle Ben is sitting in the **saddle** and holding on.

sandals In summer you can wear **sandals** without socks.

sandwich The **sandwich** is cut into four parts.

scarf Nancy wears a **scarf** to keep warm.

scary The house on the hill looks **scary**.

seat belt In our family's car, everyone must wear a **seat belt**.

secret Ann keeps her special things in a **secret** place.

share Jeff and Jody **share** the toys.

shovel It is Jeff's turn to use the **shovel**.

skyscraper A **skyscraper** is a building so tall that it scrapes the sky.

snail There are three fish and a **snail** in the bowl.

soup Larry likes alphabet **soup** best.

slipper Rover took Sharon's other **slipper**.

smiling Sharon is not **smiling** at Rover.

spaghetti It is not easy to eat **spaghetti**.

spider Along came a **spider** and sat down beside Miss Muffet.

squirrel Tom feeds nuts to the **squirrel**.

sponge A soapy **sponge** makes you clean.

stairs The baby can climb up the **stairs** but not down.

sprinkler The **sprinkler** waters the grass and Linda.

stamp Lisa has a new **stamp** for her stamp collection.

station We are waiting in the **station** for
Uncle Mike to arrive.

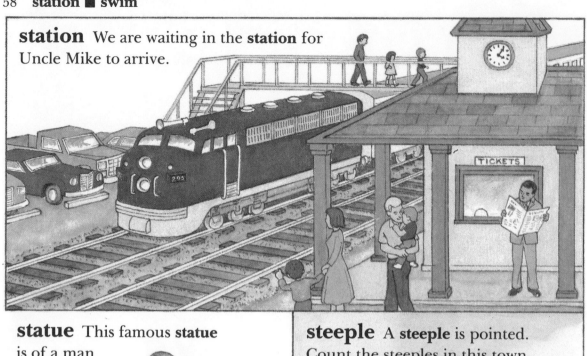

statue This famous **statue**
is of a man
who is thinking.

steeple A **steeple** is pointed.
Count the steeples in this town.

steam Boiling water
makes **steam**.

storm Skipper barks in a **storm**.

surprise Aunt Jean knitted a **surprise** for Andy.

sweater Andy likes his new sleeveless **sweater**.

sweep Mark needs to **sweep** the floor around his desk.

swim Kate can **swim** far.

Tt

temperature In summer the **temperature** outside rises.

tent Two people can fit in this **tent**.

theater Chris is going to see *Bambi* in a movie **theater.**

ticket Chris gives his **ticket** to the ticket taker.

tickle Sally likes to **tickle** Sam.

toaster You make toast in a **toaster.**

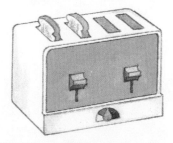

tooth Sandy lost a **tooth**.

tornado A **tornado** is a dangerous storm that is sometimes called a whirlwind or a twister.

tracks Whose **tracks** are these?

traffic light
The **traffic light** is green.
It is safe to walk.

tray Daddy brings Roy's lunch on a **tray**.

treat The ice cream is a **treat** for Roy's sore throat.

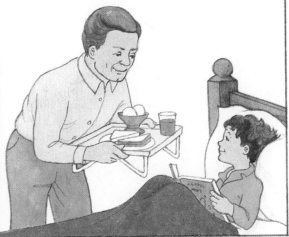

truck The **truck** is carrying chickens.

tunnel The truck is too big for this **tunnel**.

turnstile Children under five can go under the **turnstile** free.

turtle A **turtle** can hide in its shell.

Uu

umbrella Ellen carries an **umbrella** in the rain.

umpire The **umpire** called, "Strike three!"

undertow The **undertow** is strong. Don't go in the water.

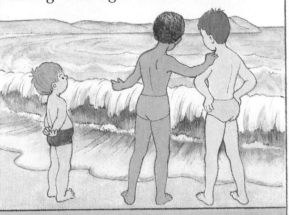

underwear The **underwear** is drying outside.

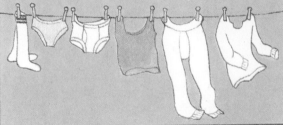

unicycle The clown can balance on a **unicycle**.

uniform For some jobs people wear a **uniform**.

United States There are 50 states in the **United States**.

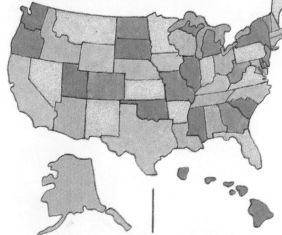

unusual Howard's socks are **unusual**.

up The balloon went **up** and **up** and **up**.

usher The **usher** is showing people where to sit.

Vv

vacuum cleaner The noise from the **vacuum cleaner** scares Kitty.

vegetable garden Joan grows tomatoes and carrots in her **vegetable garden**.

Venetian blind Some windows have a window shade and some have a **Venetian blind**.

ventriloquist The **ventriloquist** does not move his lips when the dummy talks.

vest Jerry's good suit has a jacket, pants, and a **vest**.

vine Grapes grow on a **vine**.

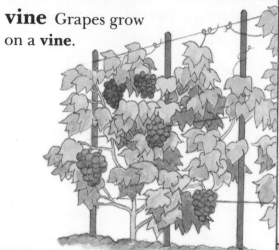

vitamin C Oranges, lemons, and grapefruits have **vitamin C**.

violin Henry is practicing the **violin**.

volcano Lava comes out of a **volcano**.

visit Betsy's cousin has come to **visit**.

Ww

wagon The farmer pulls a **wagon** full of hay.

wallet Paul keeps pictures of his family in his **wallet**.

waterfall Niagara Falls is a famous natural **waterfall**.

wedding cake The baker is decorating a **wedding cake**.

whale A **whale** is a mammal, not a fish.

wheelbarrow The pig is wheeling bricks in a **wheelbarrow**.

whistle When the lifeguard blows her **whistle**, everyone gets out of the pool.

White House The President of the United States lives in the **White House**.

windy It is hard to walk when it is **windy**.

wrapper Colleen takes the **wrapper** off the candy bar.

X x

x-ray The **x-ray** showed that Donna's wrist was not broken.

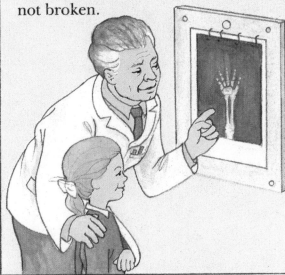

xylophone Gary is banging on a toy **xylophone**.

Y y

yarn There are different colors of **yarn** in the basket.

yelling Why is Karen **yelling**?

yellow jacket A **yellow jacket** stung her.

yolk Louis likes only the **yolk** of the egg and Beth likes only the white.

zipper Ken's **zipper** is stuck.

zoo The class took a trip to the **zoo**.

THE FIFTY STATES
AND THEIR CAPITAL CITIES

The District of Columbia is a city, not a state.
It is also called Washington, D.C. It is the capital city of the nation.

State ★ Capital City	State ★ Capital City
Alabama ★ Montgomery	**Montana** ★ Helena
Alaska ★ Juneau	**Nebraska** ★ Lincoln
Arizona ★ Phoenix	**Nevada** ★ Carson City
Arkansas ★ Little Rock	**New Hampshire** ★ Concord
California ★ Sacramento	**New Jersey** ★ Trenton
Colorado ★ Denver	**New Mexico** ★ Santa Fe
Connecticut ★ Hartford	**New York** ★ Albany
Delaware ★ Dover	**North Carolina** ★ Raleigh
Florida ★ Tallahassee	**North Dakota** ★ Bismarck
Georgia ★ Atlanta	**Ohio** ★ Columbus
Hawaii ★ Honolulu	**Oklahoma** ★ Oklahoma City
Idaho ★ Boise	**Oregon** ★ Salem
Illinois ★ Springfield	**Pennsylvania** ★ Harrisburg
Indiana ★ Indianapolis	**Rhode Island** ★ Providence
Iowa ★ Des Moines	**South Carolina** ★ Columbia
Kansas ★ Topeka	**South Dakota** ★ Pierre
Kentucky ★ Frankfort	**Tennessee** ★ Nashville
Louisiana ★ Baton Rouge	**Texas** ★ Austin
Maine ★ Augusta	**Utah** ★ Salt Lake City
Maryland ★ Annapolis	**Vermont** ★ Montpelier
Massachusetts ★ Boston	**Virginia** ★ Richmond
Michigan ★ Lansing	**Washington** ★ Olympia
Minnesota ★ St. Paul	**West Virginia** ★ Charleston
Mississippi ★ Jackson	**Wisconsin** ★ Madison
Missouri ★ Jefferson City	**Wyoming** ★ Cheyenne

THE CONTINENTS OF THE WORLD

A continent is a large area of land. There are seven continents in the world.
The biggest continent is Asia. The smallest is Australia.

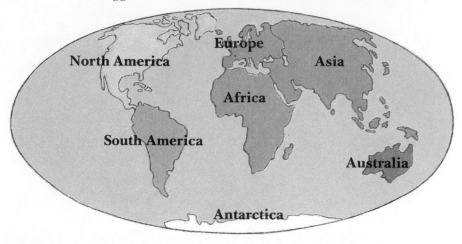

THE PLANETS OF OUR SOLAR SYSTEM

In the solar system, we know of nine planets that travel around the sun.
Our solar system is just one tiny part of the Milky Way galaxy,
which has more than 100 billion stars.

The moon is a satellite that moves around the planet Earth.

THE NINE PLANETS

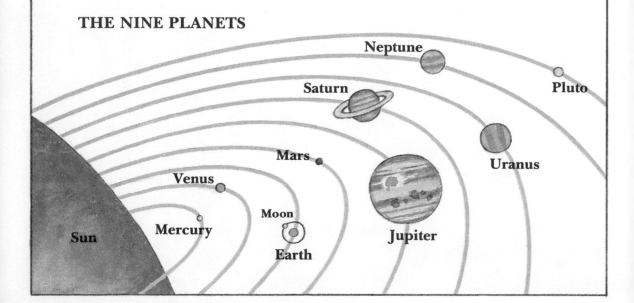